EEK! I HEAR A SQUEAK
AND THE SCURRYING OF LITTLE FEET

Written by Lavelle Carlson

Illustrated by Jenny Loehr

Eek! I Hear a Squeak
And the Scurrying of Little Feet
Copyright 2006

Written by Lavelle Carlson
Illustrated by Jenny Loehr

Inquiries should be addressed to:
Children's Publishing
201 Woodland Park
Georgetown, Texas 78628

First Edition

ISBN-13: 978-0-9725803-8-0
ISBN-10: 0-9725803-8-7

Library of Congress Catalog Card Number: 2006903802

Publishers Cataloging-In-Publication:

Carlson, Lavelle.
    Eek! I hear a squeak and the scurrying of little feet / written by
    Lavelle Carlson ; illustrated by Jenny Loehr.
    1st ed.
    28 p. : col. ill. ; 28 cm. + 1 CD-ROM (sd., col. ; 4 3/4 in).
    Summary: When Kid goes to bed and can't sleep because he hears
    a squeak, Papa Billy and Mama Nanny goat try to find it, and Kid insists
    that he wants to actually see it. Interactive storybook and compact disc with
    sound and pictures.
    Intended audience: Preschool-Primary grades.
    ISBN: 9780972580380 (hardcover : alk. paper)
    (10-digit): 0972580387 (hardcover : alk. paper)

1. Goats—Juvenile fiction. 2. Animal sounds—Juvenile fiction.
3. Reading (Preschool). 4. Basal reading instruction. 5. Stories in rhyme.
[1. Goats—Fiction. 2. Animal sounds—Fiction. 3. Stories in rhyme.]
I. Loehr, Jenny, ill. II. Title. III. Title: I hear a squeak and the scurrying
of little feet.

[E] 22
CIP: TxGeoBT   2006903802

Printed in Hong Kong

1

3

4

8

10

11

15

SQUEAK SQUEAK SQUEAK

17

19

23

The End!